This book belongs to:

Steve
-Dinosaur-

Diggory Doo
-Dragon-

Dazzle D
-Unicorn-

Different is NOT Bad
Dinosaur and Friends - Volume 4
by Steve Herman

ISBN: 978-1-64916-091-1 (paperback)
ISBN: 978-1-64916-092-8 (hardcover)

www.MyDragonBooks.com

First Edition: January 2021
10 9 8 7 6 5 4 3 2 1

Different is NOT BAD

Dinosaur and Friends – Volume 4

Steve Herman

Everyone can be himself –
There is nothing wrong
With liking different things –
We still can get along

We call this DIVERSITY –
When differences **unite** us –
We celebrate that we're unique
And don't let that divide us.

Dinosaur and Friends Series

My Unicorn Books Series

Get your Free Gift at www.MyDragonBooks.com/dinosaur

My Dragon Books Series

Made in United States
Troutdale, OR
04/26/2025

30894964R00026